Time
AND AGAIN

Rob Childs

Time
AND AGAIN

by a click of the clock
you can go in reverse
time and again
for better or worse

Illustrated by Nicola Slater

A & C Black • London

Reprinted 2006
First published 2005 by
A & C Black Publishers Ltd
38 Soho Square, London, W1D 3HB

www.acblack.com

Text copyright © 2005 Rob Childs
Illustrations copyright © 2005 Nicola Slater

The rights of Rob Childs and Nicola Slater to be identified as the
author and illustrator of this work have been asserted by them in
accordance with the Copyrights, Designs and Patents Act 1988.

ISBN 0-7136-7420-2
ISBN 978-0-7136-7420-0

A CIP catalogue for this book is available from the British Library.

All rights reserved. No part of this publication may be reproduced
in any form or by any means – graphic, electronic or mechanical,
including photocopying, recording, taping or information storage
and retrieval systems – without the prior permission in
writing of the publishers.

A & C Black uses paper produced with elemental chlorine-free
pulp, harvested from managed sustainable forests.

Printed and bound in Great Britain by Bookmarque Ltd, Croydon
Dorset County Library	
Askews & Holts	2014
	£4.99

CHAPTER ONE
Time to Go

'Fetch, Tan!'

Becky threw the stick across the field and the collie dog raced after it, barking in excitement. This was Tan's favourite game. She swooped onto the stick, picking it cleanly out of a clump of grass, and ran back with her prize.

'That didn't go very far,' laughed Chris. 'Girls can't throw!'

'OK, so you can throw better than me, little brother,' Becky said, teasing her twin with a gentle reminder, as she often did, that she was ten minutes older. 'But I can run faster.'

Chris didn't argue with that. His sister could outsprint everybody in their class.

'Let me have a go,' he said, taking the stick

from Tan's mouth. 'Bet I can reach the river from here.'

The stick whirled through the air with the dog yelping after it and both ended up in the water. Tan soon scrambled out onto the bank with her prize clamped between her teeth and shook herself, spraying thousands of droplets into the air.

'We'd better make our way back home,' said Becky, hearing the church clock strike four times. 'Come, Tan!'

The dog bounded towards them, ears pinned back, bright eyes shining beneath the tan patches of fur that inspired her name.

Keeping well away from the railway line that snaked around the village of Barnwell, the twins continued to play stick until they went past a farmyard and Chris slipped Tan onto the lead.

'Finish, Tan,' he told her. 'Walk heel.'

Tan reluctantly obeyed, but tried to tug Chris along a little quicker than he wanted to go. There was some schoolwork waiting for him at home and he was in no hurry to get back.

'Let's just have a look round the market,'

he suggested.

Becky turned to stare at him. 'Since when have you been interested in traipsing round the Sunday market?'

Chris ran a hand through his tousled fair hair, a sure sign that he was a little uncomfortable. 'Well, you never know what you might find.'

'No, but I know *you* all right,' said Becky with a grin. 'You haven't done that homework yet, have you?'

Chris shrugged. That was the trouble with having a twin sister. She always seemed to know what he was thinking. 'No sweat,' he grunted in response. 'Got plenty of time after tea.'

'No, you haven't. You promised Dad you'd help him restock the shelves, ready for tomorrow.'

Chris groaned. He'd forgotten about that. The Jackson family ran the village store and their parents were keen that the twins should 'do their bit', as Mum put it.

'Can't you do it tonight, sis?' he whined.

'No, it's your turn. I did *my bit* earlier, cleaning the counters.'

He let out a heavy sigh. 'Oh, well – all the more reason for not rushing back, then. C'mon, let's check out that market.'

They made their way to the village square, where most of the traders were already beginning to pack their unsold wares into boxes, bags and crates. As Becky paused at a clothes stall, Chris spotted a familiar, dark-haired figure slouching towards them and cursed under his breath.

He saw enough of Luke at school. They sat at the same table in class, though not by choice. Mum had caught Luke trying to pinch sweets from the store more than once and called him a born troublemaker. She was probably right too.

'Fancy meeting *you* here!' Chris greeted him, pulling a face. 'Come to see what you can nick, have you?'

'I don't nick stuff,' Luke protested.

'Oh yeah? Since when?'

'Shove off, Jacko – and take that ugly mutt with you.'

'Tan's beautiful,' said Becky, giving her a little pat.

'I wasn't talking about the dog,' cackled Luke, delighted his joke had worked so well.

Chris's reaction caught Luke off guard. He pushed him in the chest so hard that Luke stumbled back against one of the stalls, making it wobble. Luke had no chance to fight back, even if he had dared, as a snarling Tan was now standing in front of Chris.

'Oi! Clear off!' shouted the stallholder. 'Don't want you lot muckin' about round 'ere, disturbin' my customers.'

'What customers?' snorted Luke, casting an eye over the clutter of items on the bric-a-brac stall. 'Who'd want to buy any of this rubbish?'

'Cheeky brat!' the man stormed, getting off his chair. He was much bigger than Luke had realised. 'I'll have you.'

Luke shot a threat at Chris too. 'And I'll have you at school tomorrow, Jacko – when your dog's not around to protect you.' He turned and snatched the nearest thing that came to hand off the stall and then ran out of the market.

'Oi! Come back 'ere with that watch!' the man cried, but Luke was already lost to sight.

So was Becky. Still annoyed by Luke's insult, she had hared off in pursuit, closely followed by Tan, who had yanked the lead out of Chris's grasp.

It was a little while before Chris caught up with them all. Guided by the noise of Tan's barking, he found them in an alleyway, where Luke had tried to hide behind a large rubbish bin. Becky was too quick to be fooled, however, and she had also managed to seize the end of the lead to keep Tan in check.

When Chris arrived on the scene, Luke dropped the watch into the bin. 'You want it, you get it,' he told the twins. 'I'm off.'

Luke gave Tan a wide berth, but brushed past Chris, deliberately making physical contact, shoulder-to-shoulder, as he lurched along the alley.

Chris looked at his sister. 'You or me?' he said, knowing the answer.

'You,' Becky grinned. 'I've got Tan.'

Chris opened the lid of the bin. 'Phhwwaahh! It stinks in there!'

It was just as well, perhaps, that the bin was fairly full as it would have been difficult – and very unpleasant – to reach right down to the bottom.

'Wish I was wearing gloves,' he muttered, then held his breath while he rummaged carefully among the bin's rotting contents.

'Any luck?' asked Becky.

Chris grunted a response, just as his hand closed upon what felt like a chain. He pulled it out to discover that it was attached to a silver watch.

'Result!' he cried in triumph, dangling the watch above Tan's quivering nose.

11

Becky took it from him, using her sleeve to wipe some mess off the glass. 'Looks a bit like a stopwatch with these buttons around the dial,' she said. 'Must be quite old, though. It's even got Roman numerals.'

'Didn't think the Romans had watches,' Chris grinned. 'Probably had to lug sundials round with them if they wanted to know the time!'

Becky turned the watch over in the palm of her hand and saw there was some writing on the back. It was in the form of a short rhyme, although the small squiggly script made it quite awkward to read.

by a click of the clock
you can go in reverse
time and again
for better or worse

'Strange,' she murmured. 'Wonder what that means?'

'Search me,' said Chris, leaning on her shoulder to peer at the verse himself. 'I'm no good at poetry.'

'*By a click of the clock*,' she repeated. 'Hmm, well let's try this button at the top first and see what happens.'

Becky pressed down the red button above the XII...

Click!

...and was struck dumb.

They were both standing in the field by the river again, with Tan demanding the stick to be thrown for her to fetch.

The twins stared at each other in disbelief. The only thing that was different from before was that Becky now had a watch in her hand.

'What the hell are we doing back here?' Chris muttered. 'This is crazy!'

CHAPTER TWO
Time Slip

'I don't … understand,' Becky said shakily. 'What's happened, Chris?'

'Dunno,' he said. 'Makes no sense.'

Only Tan appeared unaffected, and just wanted to play.

'Finish, Tan,' Chris ordered, to stop her barking. 'Quiet!'

Tan whimpered a protest or two and then lay in the long grass, tongue lolling out of the side of her mouth. Becky sat down next to her, feeling a little dizzy. She stroked Tan's smooth black coat and white neck frill, as much to seek some reassurance for herself as to comfort the dog. She needed to know that this was for real and not a dream – or a nightmare.

'Good girl,' she said. 'It's OK.'

'It's not OK,' Chris grunted. 'It's not even close to OK. We're supposed to be in the village, not in the middle of a field!'

Becky looked at the watch. 'Last thing I remember doing was pressing this red button...'

'Well don't do it again,' said Chris, fearing that she might. 'Give it to me.' He reached out for the watch, but Becky refused to hand it over.

'*By a click of the clock,*' she murmured, repeating the first part of the inscription, '*you can go in reverse...*'

Chris shrugged. 'So?'

'So that's what we seem to have done – gone backwards in time,' said Becky, her eyes wide. 'And here we are by the river again.'

Chris stared into the distance towards the clock on the church tower.

'It's only half-past three,' he pointed out. 'And we heard it strike four earlier, remember?'

'You mean *later*,' Becky corrected him. 'It hasn't actually happened yet.'

Chris slumped to the ground beside his twin. This was all too much to take in.

Tan immediately came to try and lick his face, but he pushed her away. 'Daft dog! Get down.'

'Don't take it out on Tan,' said Becky. 'She's only wanting some fuss. She doesn't know what's going on.'

'Well that makes three of us, then.'

'We must have slipped back about an hour,' said Becky, 'but things are not exactly the same, are they? For a start, we weren't having this conversation before.'

'No, and I wasn't getting a wet bum, sitting in this grass,' Chris replied, standing up and wiping the seat of his jeans. 'C'mon, let's go.'

Becky didn't budge. She was examining the watch again and had noticed a separate dial in the lower left quarter of the face. Inside was a little gold arrow that was glowing – and slowly on the move. 'Look at this,' she said, holding out the watch for her brother to take. 'There's a tiny extra hand – and I bet it's ticking off the past hour.'

Chris held the watch to his ear. 'Can't hear any ticking.'

'You know what I mean. That red button must have set it off.'

'Guess you're right,' he conceded. 'So what do we do now?'

Becky considered the situation for a few moments. 'Well, first thing we should do is go back to the market and return this watch. It's not ours.'

'No, not yet – but it will be.'

'How?'

'We'll buy it.'

'Oh no we won't,' Becky protested,

jumping to her feet in alarm. 'I think it's too dangerous…'

'Rubbish!' he snorted, refusing to listen to her concerns.

Chris strode away towards the village, keen to reach the market before Luke appeared. He had no idea how this whole time-slip business worked, but he did know one thing for sure. He wanted that watch.

'Hold on! Hold on!' Becky cried, jogging along with Tan to catch him up.

'What's the matter now?' he said sharply.

'Have you really thought this through?'

'What do you mean?'

'What I mean is, how can you buy something that isn't there?' she reasoned. 'The chap probably doesn't even know it's missing yet.'

That made Chris stop and think, ruffling his hair in agitation.

'Well, guess we'll just have to smuggle it back onto his stall first,' he replied, 'and then buy it.'

Against her better judgement, Becky agreed to play her part in Chris's ruse, distracting the stallholder with a question about one of the items for sale while Chris pretended to lift the watch from out of a box.

'Er … how much is this?' he asked.

''ow much you got, kid?'

Chris fished into the pocket of his jeans to see what was left of his pocket money and produced a two-pound coin.

'Is that enough?' he asked hopefully.

The man shook his head. 'But make it three and it's yours.'

Chris looked pleadingly towards Becky, who sighed and gave him the extra pound.

'That's only a loan,' she insisted. 'I want it back next week.'

'Thanks, sis,' he grinned. 'You won't regret it.'

'Huh!' she grunted. 'Famous last words.'

Chris paid the money and dragged his twin and Tan away from the stall before the man could change his mind.

'What a bargain!' Chris giggled. 'He obviously hasn't got a clue what this watch can do!'

'No, and nor have we,' Becky argued. 'We don't know what we might be messing with.'

'Messing with?'

'Yes, messing with Time – with a capital T,' she told him. 'It's asking for Trouble. And that's got a capital T too!'

CHAPTER THREE
Time is Money

'Look lively, lad. You're half asleep.'

'Sorry, Dad,' Chris said automatically. He seemed to spend most of his time at home apologizing to his parents.

'Got something on your mind, have you?'

Chris smiled to himself. He could hardly try to explain about the Timewatch, as he had begun to call it. He was so keen to use it again, it was almost burning a hole in his pocket.

'Er … just some work I've still got to do for school, Dad,' he said as an excuse, glad that the watch could now give him any extra time he might need.

'Aye, well, you should've done it earlier like your sister.'

'Sorry, Dad.'

21

'Now get those tins finished and then put the cereal boxes over there,' Dad told him, pointing to an empty shelf on the other side of the store.

Chris continued to stack the tins of soup, tomatoes and baked beans on the shelf behind the main counter, ensuring that all the labels were facing the front.

'If folk can't see it, they can't buy it,' Dad always said. 'Second law of shopkeeping.'

Dad had lots of these laws and was quick to remind Chris of them whenever the chance arose. Chris deliberately put a tin of chicken soup the wrong way round to see how long it would take his father to notice.

'Come and give us a hand a minute, lad. Need you to hold these steps steady while I tidy that top shelf.'

'I don't know why we have stuff right up there. Nobody can reach it.'

'No, but I can with the steps. All they need do is point. What's the fifth law?'

Chris did a quick check down his mental list of laws. 'Er … if folk want it, we get it – right?'

'Right, good lad,' Dad beamed, putting his

weight on the rickety wooden stepladder and climbing halfway up.

'Isn't it about time we got some new steps, Dad? These always wobble.'

'If they were good enough for your old grandad, they're good enough for me,' Dad told him, starting to take the cartons off the shelf one by one, give each a rub with a cloth and then put them back in exactly the same place.

Chris wondered idly how many of the ever-growing list of laws had been passed on by Grandad. He gave a yawn and thought he might make his own list of things to do with the Timewatch. That would be a very long list as well…

…he could use it in class to redo a test and put right any mistakes…

…and double the time of his favourite PE sessions…

…and even replay a football match if his school team were losing…

…and then at home he could perhaps delay bedtime by an hour…

'Aaargh!'

Dad's shout and the crash of the steps

brought Becky, Mum and a barking Tan rushing into the store. Tan reached Dad even before Chris could scramble over the broken tangle of wood. She was yelping in alarm and trying to lick the man's face as he lay on the floor behind the counter.

'Are you all right, Dad?' cried Chris, pushing Tan away.

Dad groaned as his wife propped him up against a cabinet for support. 'Think I've gone and bust a leg,' he grunted, his face screwed up in pain.

'Whatever happened?' asked Mum, her own face white with shock.

'It was my fault,' Chris admitted. 'I wasn't holding the steps properly.'

'Nonsense, lad,' said Dad. 'You were right. They're too old. Should've got rid of 'em years ago.'

Becky crouched beside her father, stroking his arm for comfort and gripping Tan by her collar to keep the dog at bay.

'What were you doing, Dad?' she asked.

'Stretching too far, lass. Overreached myself and down I went.'

'I'm really sorry, Dad,' said Chris, as Mum went off to phone for an ambulance.

'Nothing you could have done, lad. Even if you *were* half asleep!'

'Maybe not,' Chris murmured. 'But there *is* something I can do now.' He took out the Timewatch and glanced at his sister, who nodded her approval.

Click!

Chris suddenly found himself on his own in the stockroom an hour earlier. He gave a little shake of the head in wonder and put the watch back in his pocket. Then he picked up a box of soup tins to take into the store, knowing exactly what Dad was about to say.

'Get started on those tins, lad. Time is money, remember. Third law. I don't want to be here all night.'

'No, and I bet you don't want to spend it in hospital either,' Chris muttered under his breath.

As Chris set about his tasks again, he was planning how to prevent the accident. But he still remembered to put the tin of soup the wrong way round to test his father's powers of observation. He also took the chance to go and tell Becky about the steps, realising that this time she had not travelled back in time with him for some reason.

'Why didn't you come with me?' he said, almost accusingly.

'I didn't even know you'd gone,' she retorted. 'It hasn't happened yet.'

Chris nodded slowly. It all seemed very confusing. 'Anyway, it just shows how useful this watch is,' he said. 'Y'know, the way it can let us stop people getting hurt, for instance.'

'Of course,' she agreed. 'So long as we do only use it in emergencies.'

'Depends what you mean by emergencies.'

Becky looked at him suspiciously. 'And just what do *you* mean, little brother?'

Chris turned away to avoid having to confess all the things that would be added to his list – like having enough time to finish his homework, for a start.

Dad's own work was interrupted by the occasional customer coming in for drinks or items of food that had run low over the weekend.

'Just sold Mrs Brown that loaf I thought I'd have to throw out,' he chuckled. 'Her old man's going to get some stale sandwiches in his packed lunch tomorrow.'

'You didn't have to sell it,' Chris said, knowing the answer.

'First law of shopkeeping, lad. The customer is always right,' Dad said and then gave a grin. 'Even when they're wrong. Business is business.'

Having worked a little quicker this time

around, Chris was already dealing with the cereal boxes when Dad called him over to help.

'Come and give us a hand a minute, lad. Need you to hold these steps steady while I tidy that top shelf.'

'Isn't it about time we got some new steps, Dad?' Chris said for the second time.

'If they were good enough for your old grandad, they're good enough for me.'

That was the cue for Chris to take decisive – and dramatic – action. Before his dad could mount the steps, he jumped up onto them and deliberately made them wobble.

'Be careful!'

Dad's warning was to no avail. The steps tottered and then collapsed, but Chris was ready, leaping off and rolling away across the floor so they wouldn't land on top of him. The crash brought everyone running, as before, and a noisy, nosy Tan was soon on the scene, licking Chris's face.

'Get off, daft dog,' he cried, struggling to get up.

'Are you all right?' asked Dad anxiously as Mum fussed over him too.

'I'm OK,' Chris insisted, putting on a brave act, but slipping Becky a sly wink. 'Just a few bruises in the morning, I expect, that's all.'

'What on earth were you doing?' said Mum.

'Just *doing my bit*,' he said. 'Y'know, trying to help Dad, like.'

'Aye, well,' Dad sighed. 'You were probably right about those old steps. Should've got rid of 'em years ago.'

'I've been telling you that, too,' said Mum. 'If it'd been you falling off them, you might have broken your neck.'

'Or a leg,' put in Becky. 'Dead easy!'

'Right, come into the kitchen, Chris,' Mum told him, 'and let me have a look at that arm, just to make sure there's no real damage done.'

'Oh, just one thing before you go, lad.'

'What's that?'

'Put that tin of soup the right way round, will you.'

Chris grinned. 'Sorry, Dad.'

CHAPTER FOUR
Extra Time

'What's this?'

'Er … it's my homework, Mr Samuels,' said Chris.

The teacher held up the dirty, crumpled sheets of paper for the rest of the class to see. 'It looks like something the dog's dragged in.'

Chris reddened as he felt all eyes turn towards him, with Luke's laughter louder than anyone's. The teacher wasn't far wrong. It was true that Tan's wet paws had walked over the top page that morning when it had fallen onto the floor at home, but the real damage had been done by Luke.

As Chris had been sorting through the pages in the classroom, hoping that Mr Samuels would not mind the paw prints too much – and perhaps even make a joke of it –

Luke had snatched the sheets from him, screwed them up and then tossed them into the waste bin.

'Sorry, Mr Samuels,' Chris said, running a hand through his hair. He had no intention of telling tales. He wasn't like that, as Luke knew only too well.

'I should think so, too, Christopher,' said the teacher. 'But I'm afraid being sorry isn't enough. You will have to stay in at lunch and write this out all over again.'

Luke sniggered. 'Serves you right, Jacko,' he hissed across the table. 'And I haven't finished with you yet.'

Chris glanced across the room at Becky. She was about the only one not smiling at his discomfort. He wished now that she hadn't persuaded him to leave the Timewatch at home.

'Who wants to have an extra hour of school?' she had said to convince him that she was right.

It was a fair point, but he could have gone back an hour and made sure that Luke had no chance to get him into trouble. Now he would have to miss the lunch-time game of football in the playground.

Chris tried to keep a low profile for the rest of the morning, not wanting to attract the attention of his teacher again. Luke, however, had other ideas. He kicked Chris under the table, making him yelp in pain and surprise.

'Was that you making that noise, Christopher?' demanded the teacher.

'Sorry, Mr Samuels.'

'*Sorry, Mr Samuels,*' mocked Luke out of the corner of his mouth.

'Then please be quiet. Some people here are trying to work.'

Luke sniggered. 'Not exactly Sammy's blue-eyed boy this morning, are you, *Christopher*?' He kicked out again but Chris was ready for him, grabbing Luke's foot and yanking him off his chair.

Mr Samuels put the blame on Luke this time. 'You can join Christopher in here at lunch,' he told him, 'and get on with that Maths you haven't done yet.'

Becky drifted by their table a few minutes later on her way to the other side of the room to return a book to a shelf. 'You boys having fun together?' she said, smiling.

Luke swore at her, but she kept smiling. She was also keen to carry out her own little act of revenge for yesterday's insult in the market. On the way back to her seat, via the sink, she passed behind Luke and tipped some water down the back of his neck.

She sat down at her own table, the very picture of innocence, and resumed her work while Luke's loud complaints went unheeded by the teacher.

The running feud continued throughout the day.

When Mr Samuels left the room briefly,

he returned to find the two boys brawling on the floor and gave them both extra work to do at home. During the afternoon, he had to stop them flicking pencils at each other across the table and then he caught Luke and Becky squabbling over the use of some science apparatus.

The teacher's patience finally ran out and he sat all three in separate corners of the room with strict orders not to move for the rest of the session.

Despite their differences, the trio still took part as usual in the after-school football practice. Surprisingly, Mr Samuels seemed pleased to see them, but that might have been because Luke was the team's top scorer that season.

The squad was divided into four groups for a series of five-a-side games and Luke was delighted to find himself playing against Chris in the first match.

'Sucker for punishment, ain't yer, Jacko,' he sneered. 'Always coming back for more. When you gonna realise you're useless in goal?'

The criticism stung. Chris would have

been the first to admit that the regular first-team goalie, Butch, was better than him, but he certainly wasn't useless. And neither was he in the mood for any more cheek from Luke.

'Well you won't score against me in this game,' he boasted.

Luke laughed. 'We'll see about that.'

Both boys were determined to outdo the other. Chris was in inspired form, saving everything that Luke's team could fire at him, but Luke was perhaps guilty of trying too hard to score.

'Don't be greedy,' called Mr Samuels when Luke shot straight at Chris from a narrow angle. 'You should have passed to somebody in a better position.'

Luke scowled. The only thing that mattered right now was that he should put the ball past Chris himself and time was running out. Much to his relief, and Chris's dismay, the striker finally managed to poke the ball into the net from close range beneath the keeper's desperate dive.

'One-nil!' Luke cried. 'The winner!'

And so it proved, with Luke taking great

delight in taunting Chris further before the teams swapped around to play new opponents.

'Right, that does it,' Chris muttered under his breath. 'I really will come back for more now. We're going to play extra time!'

He excused himself from the practice, telling his teacher that he was not feeling very well. As soon as he was out of sight, though, Chris broke into a run and didn't stop until he reached home. Fortunately, his parents were busy in the store and he was able to enter the house through the back garden, fuss Tan and slip up to his room to collect the Timewatch from the top drawer of his bedside cabinet.

To save his energy, Chris did not bother to hurry back to school. He simply pressed the red button...

Click!

...and transported himself back through time by one hour.

'Hmm, perhaps that wasn't a great idea,' he mused, finding himself sitting in a corner of the classroom again. 'Should've left it a bit longer.'

During the warm-up routine at the start of football practice, Chris managed to snatch a few words with Becky.

'I'm back,' he said.

'What?' she replied, concentrating on her stretching exercises. 'You've not been anywhere.'

'Yes, I have. I've been home.'

She realised what that meant. 'I thought we agreed not to bring that thing,' she said crossly.

'I needed it for an action replay,' he said, grinning.

Sadly for Chris, the grin was soon wiped off his face. Having exchanged words with Luke, as before, the game followed a different pattern after Chris himself went and changed the script in the very first minute.

When the striker tried a hopeful, long-range drive, Chris had already moved into position to repeat his earlier save. This time, however, perhaps through over-confidence, he was too casual and allowed the ball to squirm from his grasp and over the line.

'One-nil!' cried Luke. 'Easy!'

Chris held his head in his gloved hands in

horror. He could not believe what he had just gone and done. 'That wasn't supposed to happen!' he wailed miserably.

The mistake proved costly. Boosted by the goal, their opponents played with greater confidence and Chris had to pick the ball out of the net three more times in a 4–1 defeat. And to add to Chris's misery, Luke even scored a hat trick.

'Told you, Jacko,' he gloated. 'You're useless in goal!'

Chris shook his head in dismay, recalling the final line of the rhyme on the back of the Timewatch, and realising it could indeed work out both ways...

...for better *or worse.*

CHAPTER FIVE
Time for Action

'Can't say I didn't warn you, little brother,' Becky chuckled as they strolled along the bank of the river after tea. 'Serves you right!'

Chris shrugged and tossed a stick into the early evening mist for Tan to fetch.

'Just unlucky, that's all,' he grunted. 'Anybody can have an off day.'

'Yes, but they don't normally want to make it last even longer, do they?'

Chris nodded. 'Fair enough,' he conceded, half wishing that he hadn't told his twin about using – or misusing – the Timewatch to replay a game of football. 'I've learnt my lesson. I won't do it again.'

By contrast, Becky was in a good mood after scoring a goal in each of her own team's matches. The best was a left-footed volley which had flown past Chris into the top corner of the net. He would not be allowed to forget that for quite some time.

'I'm glad you didn't try to wipe out my goal,' she said, grinning.

'Couldn't be bothered by then,' he muttered. 'I was past caring.'

They were quiet for a while, lost in thought, and only Tan's excited barking disturbed the peaceful atmosphere by the river. She seemed to have picked up the scent of some creature and was following its trail.

'Weird, the way things can change,' Chris said suddenly. 'Y'know, how they can work out differently, if you have a second chance – like recording over something else on a tape.'

Becky considered that for a few moments and then sighed. 'Well, you can only do what you think is right at the time, even if that turns out to be wrong,' she said. 'Life's not a dress rehearsal. It's the real thing.'

'Is it? I'm not so sure any more,' Chris replied doubtfully and then switched his attention towards the farm on the edge of the village. 'Now that's what I call a big bonfire. Just look at those flames!'

Becky stared through the mist. 'The farmer must know what he's doing.'

'Not if his daughter's anything to go by,' Chris said with a smirk. 'She isn't nicknamed Zany Zoe for nothing.'

'Zoe's all right really, she's just a bit...' Becky paused, struggling to find the right adjective to describe Zoe's somewhat eccentric behaviour at school, '...scatty, that's all.'

'*Scatty*!' Chris scoffed. 'She makes even Luke seem sensible – almost.'

'Let's go to the farm and see if she's around.'

'Why? I didn't know you two were mates.'

'We're not,' Becky said. 'I just want an excuse to go and stand near that bonfire and get warm.'

As the twins neared the farm, however, the flames were shooting up even higher and they could hear people shouting and the noise of frightened animals.

'They might need help,' Becky cried. 'C'mon – run!'

Chris managed to grab Tan and put her on the lead to stop her chasing after his sister.

By the time he entered the farmyard, the fire was out of control and had spread to the barn. He could make out two or three figures trying to douse the flames with hoses, but their efforts seemed to be having little effect.

Becky came racing back. 'We've got to do something,' she gasped. 'Have you still got the watch?'

'Sure,' said Chris, fishing it out of his coat pocket.

'Well use it. Sounds like there are animals trapped in the barn.'

'Is Zoe there?'

'No idea,' she admitted, seizing his sleeve to urge him into action. 'Just press that red button.'

Click!

The next thing they knew, they were staring at each other in surprise across the kitchen table, feeling strangely disorientated.

'Come on, you two, eat up,' Mum told them, bustling by to go into the store and help serve the customers. 'You must both be starving after all that running about, playing football.'

Becky looked down at her half-eaten meal

of sausages and beans on toast and pushed the plate away. She had lost her appetite.

'What are we doing back here?' she said.

'Having our tea – again,' Chris replied through a mouthful of food. 'If you don't want yours, I'll have it.'

'How can you eat at a time like this? The farm's on fire!'

Chris shook his head and reached for her plate. 'Not yet, it isn't, sis,' he corrected her, jabbing his fork at the kitchen clock and dropping a few beans onto the floor, which Tan licked up. 'Got plenty of time.'

'Hi, guys!' Zoe greeted them, before throwing more wood onto the small bonfire in the farmyard. 'What brings you here?'

'Er…' Chris began lamely, not quite sure how to respond, having arrived at the farm a little early. 'We were just out walking the dog and … er…'

'And doing a bit of jogging to keep fit,' added Becky in support.

'A dog jog!' Zoe cackled.

'Not exactly,' muttered Chris. 'Er … so where is everybody?'

'*Everybody*?' repeated Zoe. 'Everywhere, I guess. Why?'

'Just wondered who's supposed to be looking after this bonfire.'

'What's it look like, Jacko?' she sneered. 'Me!'

'Do your folks know?'

Zoe stared at him. 'Course they do. They don't call me zany here, y'know.'

Becky attempted to come to his rescue. 'I'm sure you know what you're doing, Zoe,' she said. 'But isn't it dangerous having a bonfire so close to the barn?'

Zoe lost patience with their questions. 'Clear off, will yer,' she snapped, striding away towards her bike which was propped up against the barn. 'I'm busy.'

The twins left the farm but did not stray far.

'So what do we do now?' asked Chris.

'We wait,' said Becky. 'I mean, we know what's going to happen, if we just leave her to it. We'll wait a while and then move in.'

'I don't want to hang about here in the cold. Let's go and sort it out now.'

'Hold on!' Becky cried. 'What will we say to Zoe? Tell her she's going to set fire to the whole place? She'll just laugh at us.'

'So what? Better than frying the pigs. Come on!'

Chris marched back into the yard and was relieved that he did not have to say anything. Zoe was nowhere to be seen – and nor was her bike – but the fire was still burning brightly.

'Right, you wait here with Tan, Becky,' he said, 'and give me a shout if you spot anybody.'

'What are you going to do?'

'Put out that fire while I still can,' he said over his shoulder.

Chris trotted over to one of the outbuildings where he saw a hose connected to a tap on the wall. Checking again that no one was about, he seized his chance. He turned on the tap and ran towards the bonfire, the length of hose unravelling behind him, slithering across the yard like a giant snake.

The water began to gush out of the nozzle even before he reached the fire, drenching his jeans until he aimed it at the flames and soon extinguished them. He soaked everywhere thoroughly, trying to make sure the fire could not be relit, and then dropped the hose to the ground.

'Turn off the water!' Becky called to him, as loudly as she dared.

Chris stopped, hesitated, and then went back to the tap, expecting at any moment to be confronted by an angry Zoe or, even worse, a furious farmer. 'Done it!' he yelped in triumph. 'Let's get out of here!'

As they made their way home, they saw Zoe on her bike. At first they assumed she must be coming after them, but she turned off into one of the side streets towards the market square.

'Phew! That was close,' Chris breathed in relief. 'Bet she's on the warpath, looking for us.'

'Well she knows where we live,' Becky said. 'And it's not up there.'

'Must be going somewhere else, then,' Chris replied, realising the significance of what he'd just said. 'Hey! Bet that's how it happened before. She rode off and left the bonfire burning and – well, we know the rest.'

Becky nodded. 'Yes, but nobody else does, so let's just keep it to ourselves.'

'Sure,' he grinned. 'My lips are zipped!' He made a quick motion with his hand across his mouth as if to seal it, but then immediately spoke again. 'Pity we can't tell her what we did, though…'

He was cut short by screams and shouts in the distance.

'I think they're coming from the market square,' said Becky, changing direction. 'C'mon, let's go and check it out.'

Becky and Tan reached the square well before a more-reluctant Chris, who had no wish to run into Zoe again. Unfortunately, somebody else had already done so.

Becky recognised Zoe's bike, even though it was now buckled and lying in the gutter. She could see no sign of Zoe herself because of the milling crowd, but she soon found out what had happened.

'Zoe's been knocked over by a car!' she gasped as Chris caught up with her. 'Use the watch. We might be able to save her.'

Click!

Nothing changed. They were still in the square and could hear the wailing siren of an approaching ambulance.

'Try again!' urged Becky.

Click! Click!

'We're already locked into extra time, remember,' he said, shaking his head. 'Maybe it can't repeat the same hour twice.'

The twins stood by, helpless, as the ambulance arrived in the square and it wasn't long before they saw a stretcher being carried into the back of the vehicle.

'Sorry, Zoe,' Chris sighed. 'But at least we put the fire out for you.'

CHAPTER SIX
A Matter of Time

'Poor lass,' Mum said while the twins were having breakfast the next day. 'It's a miracle that Zoe wasn't killed, by all accounts. Somebody told us the driver must have been doing at least sixty. He ought to be locked up.'

The twins kept quiet, each lost in their own thoughts. They were glad to have prevented the fire, but still wondered whether they could have done something else to stop Zoe from being hurt.

There was a special assembly at school that morning to pray for Zoe's recovery, but it meant more to some than others.

'I saw you in assembly, Jacko,' sneered Luke outside their lockers at lunch. 'Hands tight together, eyes shut, praying like mad.'

'So? I just want Zoe to get better,' Chris retorted. 'Don't you?'

Luke shrugged in response. 'She always rode her bike like a maniac,' he muttered. 'It was only a matter of time before she got knocked over.'

Only a matter of time.

The words stung and Chris could not stop himself. He grabbed Luke by the front of his jumper and shoved him backwards against the wall.

'What do *you* know about time?' he demanded fiercely. 'Nothing!'

'What you on about, Jacko?' cried Luke, wriggling out of his grip. 'You're as mad as her.'

Chris scowled and slouched off outside to a corner of the playground. He needed more time to think and wished he hadn't left the Timewatch at home.

He was still in a bad mood that afternoon during an art and craft session. The teacher suggested to the class that they all made or painted something that he could take into hospital to show Zoe, which would perhaps cheer her up a little.

Chris's artwork, however, would not have cheered up anybody. He painted a blood-red scene of flames with stick-like figures scurrying to and fro in panic through the smoke and sparks. Then he finished it all off by pouring water over it, just as he had hosed down the bonfire at the farm.

'What on earth is that mess meant to be, Christopher?' gasped Mr Samuels as he walked between the tables, checking on progress.

'Not sure, really,' Chris said, feeling more at peace with himself now, as if the water had also quenched his own anger. 'Just putting out a fire.'

'Well,' sighed the teacher, giving Chris a strange look. 'I don't think it's quite the thing to give to Zoe, do you?'

Chris shrugged. He was not too bothered whether she saw it or not – but he liked to think it was the kind of thing that zany Zoe might well have done herself.

By contrast with her twin, Becky still felt vaguely guilty, as if the accident were somehow their fault. Her own artwork had taken the form of a *Get Well Soon* card, but it wasn't enough. She decided that the watch had to go.

'Maybe Zoe's accident wouldn't have happened if we hadn't interfered,' she said to Chris when they were discussing the situation again after tea.

'*Interfered*?' he repeated, turning up the volume on the television so that they couldn't be overheard from the store. 'You mean, do nothing and let the farm burn down?'

'No, course not, but…'

'There you are, then,' he said, cutting her short. 'Anyway, that speeding driver might well have gone and hit somebody else instead.'

'That's just it,' she stated. 'All these possible knock-on effects of changing things – they're out of our control.'

Chris spread his hands in a helpless gesture. 'That's just down to chance – or fate,' he said. 'Being in the wrong place at the wrong time.'

'Yes, like us,' she told him. 'We've been in the wrong too, going back and trying to put things right – and perhaps making them worse.'

'So what are you suggesting?'

'Let's destroy the Timewatch!'

'What!' exclaimed Chris. 'You can't be serious.'

'I'm deadly serious. It's more trouble than it's worth. Just imagine if someone like Luke got hold of the watch and found out what it could do…'

Chris refused to listen any further. 'I'm going out,' he muttered. 'On my own.'

He went upstairs to collect the Timewatch. He wanted to take it with him for safekeeping in case Becky tried to carry out her threat. He opened the top drawer of his bedside cabinet and rummaged among his socks and hankies, but the watch wasn't there. In desperation, he threw open the other drawers, and then he began to panic.

'Becky!' he cried, thundering down the stairs. 'Where's the watch?'

He was too late.

Click!

Becky used the perfect escape route, slipping back in time, if not actually finding herself very far away. She was in the garden, playing ball with Tan again, while Chris was round at a mate's house.

'Oh, well,' she sighed, realising that their argument had not now taken place. 'At least Chris doesn't yet know that I want to get rid of this thing.'

She stared at the watch in her hand. It was very tempting to go and throw it away, but she didn't really want to do anything like that without his agreement.

'C'mon, Tan, let's go out for a little walk,' she said. 'We've got time.'

'Don't be long,' said Mum when Becky told her what she was doing. 'I'll be starting tea soon.'

Tan was in for a disappointment. It began to rain before they reached the fields and Becky decided to call on her aunt, who lived nearby, instead.

'Hello, my dear. This is a pleasant surprise,' Auntie Jean greeted her. 'Come in and I'll put the kettle on. We haven't had a good old chat for ages.'

Becky quite enjoyed her aunt's company – and her baking. A big tin of buns was placed on the table and Auntie Jean began to prepare the drinks, putting a bowl of water on the floor for Tan too.

'Can I ring Mum to let her know where I am?' Becky asked.

'Of course, my dear. The phone's in the hall.'

Becky wanted to avoid going home for another meal and told Mum that she was having tea with Auntie Jean instead, which was true up to a point – tea and buns!

When she returned to the kitchen, Auntie Jean handed her a plate. 'Do help yourself to the buns, my dear, and tell me what you've been up to recently.'

Becky was careful to make no references to the watch and confined her tales to events at school, boasting of her goals in yesterday's football practice.

'I don't know,' said her aunt, shaking her head. 'Girls playing football! It was never heard of in my day. Netball, that was my favourite game…'

Now it was Becky's turn to listen to Auntie Jean. She knew all her stories about playing for the county netball team, but was content to sit back and enjoy the buns.

When the grandfather clock struck six times, Auntie Jean put a hand to her mouth in alarm. 'Oh, my goodness!' she exclaimed. 'I've forgotten to go out and buy a ticket,'

'Ticket?'

'Yes, you know, for the *Daily Draw*.'

'Oh, right, the county lottery. It's OK, the store's still open.'

'I'm afraid it's too late now, my dear. Six o'clock is the evening deadline so they can go ahead and make the draw. Your uncle normally picks up a ticket on his way home from work, but he's doing a spot of overtime and asked me to get it today.'

'Have you ever won anything?'

'Only twenty pounds once,' Auntie Jean admitted. 'But I don't mind. Most of the money goes to support local charities and that's the main thing.'

'How much is the top prize?'

'Ten thousand pounds.'

Becky let out a low whistle. 'What would you do with all that money? Go on a world cruise or something?'

'Oh, no! Nothing so selfish, I'm sure,' she chuckled. 'We'd share our good fortune with the rest of the family. We always have the same numbers, you see, family birthdays like yours.'

The conversation moved on to other matters, including Zoe's accident, and it was only when Tan started to bark that they realised Uncle Dave had arrived home.

'Not a word to your uncle about the ticket, remember,' said Auntie Jean, pressing a finger to her lips. 'He'll never know I forgot!'

As soon as Uncle Dave walked in, Tan gave him a loud, boisterous welcome and then more drinks and food appeared, as if by magic. He switched on the radio before settling himself in his favourite armchair with the evening paper.

'Let's check whether we've won the draw!' he said, jokingly. 'You never know, Becky love, you might have brought us a bit of Lady Luck!'

Becky exchanged a furtive glance with her aunt and crossed her fingers that she hadn't done so.

There was no need for Uncle Dave to see the ticket. He knew the numbers off by heart. He was only half-listening to the radio, but as the winning numbers were read out, some of them sounded familiar enough to gain his full attention. He stared at his wife, who had turned decidedly pale, and then he jumped to his feet.

'C'mon, man!' he shouted at the radio. 'Say 'em again, will you!'

When the announcer duly obliged, repeating the five lucky numbers, Uncle Dave could hardly believe his ears. 'We've won, Jean!' he cried, giving his wife a big hug as Tan added her barks to the excitement. 'We've gone and won the thing! We've got all five numbers!'

It was some while before he had calmed down enough to allow her to break the bad news. 'I'm so sorry,' she confessed. 'With young Becky coming, I clean forgot to go and buy the ticket. Sorry!'

Her husband was so shocked, he could not even find the words to respond. He just shuffled out of the house and went into the back garden to try and swallow his disappointment. Even Tan realised that something was wrong and crouched under the table, tail between her legs.

'Not much of a Lady Luck, was I?' murmured Becky, knowing that she could not even use the watch again to repeat the past hour.

'It's not your fault, my dear,' Auntie Jean told her, forcing a false smile. 'Just one of those things.'

Becky put on her coat and trailed slowly home with Tan. She felt terrible. She knew that their loss – and hers, too, with no share of the winnings – was indeed her own fault. But she also knew what else was to blame.

It lay like a great weight in her pocket – the Timewatch.

CHAPTER SEVEN
Time Travel?

'We have to get rid of this thing,' Becky insisted, 'before it causes any more bother.'

She had forgotten to take the Timewatch out of her coat last night and now handed it over to Chris in the school playground after lunch. She wanted nothing more to do with it.

'It stops things turning out the way they were meant,' she told him.

'*Meant*?' Chris repeated, raising an eyebrow. 'Who's to know what's really meant to be?'

'We do,' she replied. 'They were meant to win the Draw and now they haven't because of that watch.'

'And you and the buns.'

'Yes, all right – and me. Go on, rub it in, little brother.'

'Hey! Less of the *little brother* stuff,' Chris retorted, grinning. 'I reckon, with our own time trips, I've lived longer than you now by about an hour – *little sister*!'

Becky pulled a face at the taunt. She almost wished she hadn't told him what had happened. She'd hoped the confession would erase some of her guilt, but she still felt wretched. Even more so, in fact, after a sleepless night. The only good news was that they had heard in assembly that Zoe was making a swift recovery.

'Let's smash it to pieces,' she suggested.

Chris plunged the watch deep into his coat pocket, in case Becky tried to snatch it back and dash it to the ground. 'We can't do that,' he stated.

'Why not?'

'Well, it might be the only watch in the world like this, that's why not. It just needs to be used properly. Y'know, to *help* people – like I did with Dad.'

Becky could hardly argue with that. She turned away to trail back inside the building, allowing Chris to join in a kickabout with some of the other boys. He needed to get involved in something physical to clear his mind.

'You can only play if you go in goal,' said Butch. 'I want to play out for a change.'

Chris was happy enough about that. He was better with his hands than his feet, even if he wasn't as good with either as Butch. He took off his coat, folded it up tightly to give the watch extra protection and placed it beneath a pile of others being used as goalposts.

Much to his own surprise, he found himself on good form, handling the ball cleanly and he even dived across the hard surface to smother one of Luke's shots.

'You see why Butch never dives on here,' Luke sneered as Chris pulled up a sleeve to examine the graze on his left elbow. 'Bet you won't do it again.'

Chris soon proved Luke wrong. He threw himself full-length to keep out another goal-bound shot and his bravery earned him applause from Butch.

'They say all goalies are crazy,' he grinned.

'Then that must include you, too,' Chris joked back.

'Guess so, but don't overdo it, Jacko. They might start thinking you're better than me!'

Chris made several more good saves but he was also beaten a few times in the high-scoring game, which finished with a victory for his team when the bell sent the players scurrying for their coats. A surly Luke chucked Chris's towards him.

'Hey!' cried Chris, catching the coat before it hit the ground. 'I've got something valuable in here.'

'What?'

'None of your business. Just *watch* it.' Chris grinned at his own pun and then brushed past Luke to head for the cloakroom. The two boys continued to bicker at their table throughout the afternoon, with the only quiet period coming when Mr Samuels gave everyone an unexpected spelling test.

What was not unexpected, however, were the poor scores of both Chris and Luke, neither of whom were exactly top of the class when it came to spelling ability.

The teacher ended the day with a story, grouping the children around him in the book corner, and it was only then that Chris realised Luke had gone missing. His suspicious mind immediately flashed to the Timewatch. He had thought about bringing it with him into class, but felt it might be safer – and less tempting to use – if he left it in the cloakroom. He was now regretting that decision – and also the stupidity of telling Luke that he had something of value in his coat.

He waved his hand in the air to attract the teacher's attention.

'What is it now, Christopher?' sighed Mr Samuels. 'I suppose you're going to tell me that time travel isn't really possible.'

Chris was taken aback. 'Sorry?' he said,

catching his twin's eye. He hadn't even been listening to the science-fiction story about people travelling through time and space. He simply wanted to leave the room.

'Well, what do you think?'

'Er…' he faltered. 'No, I'm sure it is.'

'You're *sure* it is?' repeated Mr Samuels. 'And why are you so sure?'

Becky shot Chris a warning look, fearing what he might blurt out, but she needn't have worried. Chris was too concerned about what Luke might be doing to want to be delayed by a long discussion.

'Well, I just think it must be,' he said. 'I mean…'

Chris never had the chance to say what he might have meant. 'Ow!' he winced, glaring at Luke, who had kicked him on the knee beneath their table. 'Pack it in, will you?'

For once, Luke wasn't smirking. His face had turned deathly pale.

'What's up with you?' Chris grunted, not really concerned.

'I don't know,' Luke murmured. 'Everything's gone weird – well weird…'

68

'You're well weird to start with,' Chris told him and returned to his project work.

Luke flicked a pencil at him. 'Look, Jacko, I want to know what's going on here. Don't mess me around.'

Chris stared at him. 'I've no idea what you're on about.'

Luke held out the Timewatch. 'I'm on about this thing.'

'What are you doing with that?' Chris gasped. 'Give it back.'

'Not till you tell me what's going on,' he refused. 'I just pressed this red button and then suddenly found myself back here.

It's only two o'clock – but it should be nearly home time now.'

Chris could understand Luke's confusion. He'd felt the same way himself the first time he had used the Timewatch, but he had no sympathy for him.

'That's twice you've pinched that watch,' he hissed, making a grab for it.

Luke was too quick and there was a scuffle as Chris leant over the table and tried to take it back by force.

'Stop it, you two, at once!' shouted Mr Samuels. 'Come here.'

Tempted though Chris was, as he desperately wanted the watch, he did not admit the cause of their latest dispute. The last thing he needed was for his teacher to know about the watch as well. If Mr Samuels discovered its special powers, Chris would probably never see it again. Both boys remained silent and finally, in frustration, the teacher sent them to sit in opposite corners of the room.

'Stay behind after school,' Mr Samuels told them, 'and we'll sort out this business then.'

When the teacher announced the spelling

test, only one pupil was not caught by surprise. Sitting alone, Luke had slowly come to realise what must have happened – however weird it was – and used the situation to his own advantage. Knowing which words had come up in the test before, he checked in a dictionary and tried to commit them to memory.

Mr Samuels was astonished by Luke's result. The boy had only two words wrong and he was not near enough to anybody to have copied them. 'This is remarkable, Luke,' he said. 'It shows what you are capable of when you put your mind to it. Perhaps you should sit by yourself more often.'

Luke's grin became even wider when Chris had to admit that he had spelt only half of the words right.

'A pity it's not had the same effect on you, Christopher,' said Mr Samuels, frowning at him over his spectacles.

Later on, in the book corner, when the teacher had finished reading the time-travel story, he asked the class a question:

'How many of you would like to travel back in time, if you had the chance?'

Most of the hands went up, including Luke's, which was the highest.

'Right, Luke,' said Mr Samuels, pleased to see some enthusiasm from him for a change. 'And just where might you like to go back to?'

'Not bothered,' Luke said, grinning. 'Anywhere but here.'

The children laughed, but the teacher was not amused.

'And do you think that time travel might ever be possible?' he persisted.

'It already is,' Luke claimed and he brandished the Timewatch in the air, much to the twins' horror. 'And I'll prove it – look!'

Click!

Unfortunately for Luke, he did not know that the same hour could not be repeated twice. He had made a great show of pressing the red button, but nothing happened. He clicked it again – and again – but they were still all sitting together in the book corner, staring at him as if he were mad.

'Yes, Luke, very theatrical,' the teacher drawled, unimpressed by the boy's antics. 'Perhaps we can talk about that nonsense after school, too.'

Luke slumped back against a bookcase, his face almost as red as the button on the Timewatch.

CHAPTER EIGHT
Out of Time

'So how are we going to get the watch back off Luke?' Becky voiced the question that Chris had wrestled with all the way home, after his ticking off by Mr Samuels, but he was still no nearer an answer.

'Dunno,' he muttered. 'He won't just give it back, that's for sure. He laughed at me when I asked for it outside school, and then he ran off.'

'What did Sammy say about the watch?'

'Not a lot. He didn't even ask to see it, fortunately,' Chris explained. 'He wanted to know whose it was and when Luke told him he'd borrowed it from his grandad for the day, that was it. He just told him not to bring it back into school.'

'I wonder when Luke will use the watch

again,' Becky said. 'And what he'll do?'

'First bit's easy – as soon as he can,' Chris replied. 'But as for what he'll get up to – your guess is as good as mine.'

'Right, come on. Let's go and find him,' she said, whistling for Tan to join them. 'Wherever he is.'

Luke was still at home, in fact, almost the last place the twins thought of checking. They were sure that he would be out and about, looking for mischief.

Luke had so far resisted the urge to try the red button again, suspecting that, if it worked, he might find himself suffering a repeat of his lecture from Mr Samuels. Nor did he dare press any of the other buttons around the perimeter of the watch, just in case.

'Too risky. Anything might happen,' he muttered. 'I'll wait a bit longer.'

Luke watched television for a while till he grew bored and then went into the garden to kick a ball about. It was only when a stray shot flew over the fence and broke a window in next-door's greenhouse that he decided to act – especially as their neighbour had come storming out of the house.

Click!

After a moment's blurred vision and dizziness, it seemed as though the world around him had undergone an instant scene change. He found himself back in the market square, where he had briefly been at four o'clock on his way home – exactly one hour ago.

'Well, at least that window's still in one piece, I guess,' he mused.

Luke sat on the stone steps of the statue that dominated the centre of the busy market square, wondering what to do next. That particular problem was solved by the arrival of Butch, but it only led to a far more serious one.

'What was all that nonsense in class with the watch?' asked Butch, slumping down alongside him. 'You made yourself look a right idiot.'

Luke pulled a face. He took the watch from his coat pocket and dangled it from the chain, swinging it back and forth in front of Butch's face as if trying to hypnotise him. 'Can you keep a secret?' he demanded.

Butch grinned. 'Sure.'

'Well, if you click the red button, this watch really does send you back in time.'

'Oh, yeah?' said Butch, humouring him. 'How far?'

'One hour.'

'One hour!' chortled Butch, unimpressed. 'Is that the best you can do – one measly hour?'

'Well, it's a start,' said Luke with a shrug. 'Once I get the hang of it, bet I'll be able to go back weeks – or even years.'

'Rubbish!' Butch snorted. 'Give it here.' He snatched the watch and began jabbing at the red button repeatedly. 'Nothing's happened, has it?' he scoffed. 'Nothing's changed at all.'

But something *had* happened. The button had stuck down. Butch tossed the watch back to Luke and stood up to leave.

'You've gone and broke it,' Luke wailed, desperately trying to free the button.

'Tough! I'm off.'

Butch left the market and bumped into the twins just beyond the square.

'You haven't seen Luke by any chance, have you?' asked Chris.

'Funny you should say that,' Butch replied, bending to fuss Tan. 'I've just been with him at the statue. The wally was still trying to make out that watch is some kind of time machine!'

'Does he have it with him?' asked Becky.

'Yeah – not much use now, though,' Butch chuckled. 'It's bust.'

'Bust!' exclaimed Chris.

'The red button's jammed,' he told them with a laugh, moving off. 'Serves him right, if you ask me. See ya!'

The twins looked at each other in alarm and hurried into the square. There was no sign of Luke, but they could tell where he'd been.

A fruit stall had been tipped up, causing apples and oranges to topple all over the ground, and another trader was complaining loudly that a boy had just dashed by and grabbed a handful of computer disks off his stall.

'Must be Luke,' said Chris. 'Where do you reckon he's gone now?'

'Let's try the fields,' Becky suggested. 'He might have run off there.'

To their dismay, the fields were deserted, but they extended the search along by the river until they passed a clump of trees. Chris was about to throw a stick for Tan to fetch when Becky gave a cry.

'There he is!' She was pointing towards the railway line and Chris spotted Luke, too. He was climbing over the fence on the opposite side of the track and then disappeared into an area of woodland. Chris seized Tan's collar to attach her lead while Becky set off on the chase, sprinting through the long grass and leaving them both well behind.

As Becky neared the railway, she saw what Luke had done and hesitated, turning to shout back to her brother. 'He's put a big branch on the line.'

Hardly were the words out of her mouth when they heard the loud siren of a train, a warning to anybody who might be near where the footpath crossed the single line. Trains along this stretch of track were few and far between, but Luke must have known that one was due.

Only someone of Becky's speed and agility would have been able to reach the crossing before the train. She vauleted the stile over the fence and scrunched to a halt in the gravel by the track, her heart pounding. With the train closing rapidly upon her, its noise filling her senses, she grabbed hold of the heavy branch and pulled…

Chris was still too far away to help and the long, rattling line of trucks blocked his view of the crossing point, drowning Tan's barks and his own desperate cries.

'Becky!' he screamed. 'Becky!'

CHAPTER NINE
Time Loop

Chris stared in horror over the stile as the wagons clanked by, hardly daring to think of what he might see when they had all gone past.

The sight was the one he dreaded. His sister was sprawled against the opposite fence, face down, lying very still.

'Becky!' he cried again.

To his huge relief, she slowly rolled over and sat up, her face smeared with dirt.

'I'm OK,' she croaked and then managed a lopsided grin. 'What kept you, little brother?'

Chris shook his head in bewilderment at her nerve. 'That was a stupid thing to go and do,' he told her when he and Tan had crossed the track. 'You could've got yourself killed.'

Becky scrambled to her feet, if only to escape further face-licking from Tan. 'I know. I realise that now – sorry,' she said, feeling a little weak at the knees. 'Just acted on impulse.'

'It wasn't even a passenger train.'

'Might have been,' she retorted. 'At least I saved the driver from getting hurt, if the train *had* been derailed.'

'True enough,' Chris admitted. 'Right, so let's get hold of Luke before he tries anything else like that.'

'Why would he *do* such a thing?' Becky said as they set off towards the wood where Luke had made his escape. 'It doesn't make any sense – even for him.'

There was no escape for Luke, however, from his living nightmare. With the red button jammed, he had found himself trapped in a time loop, having to keep repeating the same hour, if not the same actions. Every time the little gold arrow completed a circuit of the dial, it began to move slowly round all over again.

By the third such loop, Luke was becoming

so desperate that he had even felt tempted to stand on the line in front of the train. He panicked, though, when he heard Becky's shout and hauled the branch onto it instead.

Luke had already vented his anger and frustration in many ways. Returning to school, he scratched Mr Samuels's car with a nail, stole a football from the sports store – which he soon lost by kicking it up onto the roof – tipped over waste bins and smashed several classroom windows.

'Catch me if you can!' he yelled when the caretaker appeared on the scene – and then ran off, just in case the man gave chase.

The twins were finding Luke elusive, too, picking up his haphazard trail of vandalism in and around the village. They had no idea that he was continually on rewind and kept returning to various places…

…like the woodland, where he snapped lots of newly planted saplings…

…like the farm, where he let pigs and hens out into the yard…

…like the recreation ground, where he used school chalk to scrawl some graffiti on the wall of the changing hut…

…and like the new housing estate, where he damaged doors, flowers, trees, cars and more windows…

Finally, even Luke tired of breaking things. He went to sit by the river for a while to have a bit of a think.

'Perhaps none of it really happened,' he mused, trying to comfort himself that each extra hour served to erase what he had done before. 'Just so long as I don't get nabbed before I get out of this mess – if I ever do.'

Luke began to throw stones into the water, using a group of ducks as targets, and failed to hear the twins sneak up behind him.

'Got you at last!' Chris cried out, making Luke jump to his feet in alarm.

'What you doing here?' he grunted, in a vain effort to act cool.

'More like what were *you* doing back there on the railway line?' said Becky. 'You almost caused a train crash.'

Luke shrugged. 'Who cares?'

'We do.'

'Yeah, saw you play the big hero. What do you want?'

'The watch,' she stated simply.

Luke shrugged again. 'It's bust.'

'Yes, we know,' said Chris. 'Butch told us. But we still want it back.'

Luke took the watch from his coat pocket and glared at it. 'Thanks to Butch, I'm stuck in a kind of time warp – y'know, like in that story old Sammy was reading to us,' he said, struggling now to hold back his tears in front of the twins. 'There's no way out. I'm just going round in circles.'

In a fit of temper, Luke chucked the watch at a duck on the bank, but his aim was wild and the watch flew into the river. 'You want it – you fetch it!' he cried.

At the word *fetch* Tan darted away, as if after a stick, and plunged into the shallow water.

'Good girl!' Becky encouraged her when the dog seemed to be on the point of giving up the search. 'Fetch. Where is it?'

A few moments later, Tan's head bobbed beneath the surface and reappeared with the watch dangling from her mouth by the chain.

'Good girl!' Becky praised her again. 'Come!'

Tan doggie paddled to the bank, climbed out and shook herself vigorously – spraying Luke with water – before dropping the watch at Chris's feet.

Chris picked it up and peered at the tiny, glowing arrow. 'Must be waterproof. It still seems to be working,' he said, then pressed the red button, which refused to budge. 'Even if this isn't.'

'What time do you reach before you slip back?' Becky asked Luke.

'Five o'clock,' he muttered.

Becky glanced at her wristwatch. 'It's nearly that now,' she told Chris. 'What can we do?'

'Dunno exactly – but we've got to do something.'

He seemed to come to a decision and went to the water's edge, knelt down and scooped up a large stone from the river bed.

Luke suddenly realised what Chris had in mind. 'No! Don't, Jacko!' he yelled. 'You don't know what…'

Too late. Chris's hand came down hard, slamming the stone onto the Timewatch and breaking its glass front. The gold arrow buckled and the red button snapped back up into place.

'You nutter, Jacko!' Luke cried. 'Look what you've gone and done!'

'Just shut up and wait!' Chris told him. 'Then we'll see what I've done.'

The three of them seemed to be holding their breath and Tan wandered away to start rolling in the grass to dry her fur. After what seemed an age, the church clock began to strike the hour. They almost counted the bongs out loud.

'Right, that's five,' Chris said. 'So I reckon if anything was going to happen, Luke, you'd have been back in the market square again by now. You're free at last.'

Luke let out a sigh of relief. 'Thought about smashing the watch myself, but I didn't dare,' he admitted.

'I don't think I'd have dared either, if it'd been me,' Chris replied honestly. 'It just seemed the only thing to do.'

They stared at the broken watch on the ground.

'So what do we do with it now?' Luke asked. 'Chuck it back in the water?'

'No, we'd better destroy the Timewatch once and for all,' said Becky, taking the stone from her brother's hand. 'Make sure nobody can ever use it again.'

'Or misuse it,' added Chris, glancing at Luke.

'I'm really going to enjoy this,' Becky grinned, kneeling down. 'Been wanting to do it for ages.'

Time and again she hammered the stone onto the watch, shattering it into smithereens.

'There!' she said with satisfaction, standing up. 'Now Luke can pick up all the pieces and we can go home.'

Surprisingly, he did so without any argument, but then tossed them into the river before they could stop him.

Chris whistled for Tan and winked at his sister. 'Of course, there's still one more thing you have to do, Luke,' he said with a smirk.

'Oh, yeah – and what's that?'

'Start thinking what you might say to people about what you got up to in the last hour,' Chris told him. 'That hasn't been wiped out, remember…'

About the Author

Time travel! What a mind-bending concept it is. Just imagine having your own time machine and being able to travel back into the past – or even forwards into the future! Impossible? Well, not in the world of science fiction, one of the main areas of interest in my writing. I may be better known for all my sports stories for children, but I've written many time-travelling tales too.

Time and Again began as an idea in one of my notebooks before I let the characters loose on the page – or at least on the computer screen – and then they helped me to write the story during the drafting process.

By pressing a red button on an old watch, the children experience a time slip of one hour. Not long, maybe, but many things can happen in that extra time, especially when they are able to change what originally took place – for better or worse.

I have always enjoyed writing and had my sights set on a career in journalism after graduating from Leicester University in the early 1970s. Instead, I somehow found myself teaching in primary schools for about 20 years. The best part of the job, as far as I was concerned, was being able to run various sports clubs and coach the youngsters in a wide range of activities like football, gymnastics, cricket and athletics. It turned out to be very good experience for writing for children and I left teaching to concentrate on doing just that. I must have had about 80 books published since the first one appeared in 1980.

My wife, Joy, and I love rough collie dogs, like Lassie in the stories, and we now share our home in a Leicestershire village with one called Rocky. He always gives us a good excuse to leave our desks and enjoy walks in the local countryside and along nearby canal towpaths.

James and the Alien Experiment

Sally Prue

"The bony hand zoomed right out of the screen and grabbed him."

When James is kidnapped by aliens, he can't believe his luck. They want to transform his feeble human body and James can have whatever superpowers he likes. He chooses super-speed, super-brains and super-strength. But James soon starts to realise he might have got slightly more than he asked for…

Black Cats
Books to pounce on

Bryony Bell's Star Turn

FRANZESKA G. EWART

*"It's just as well Yours Truly has a breathtakingly
brilliant, scintillatingly surefire gem of an idea
up her sleeve."*

There's never a dull moment in the Bell
household. Fresh from success on Broadway, they
now star in their very own reality TV show. Plus
there's the mystery of Ken Undrum's long lost
love to solve, the Nativity play to rehearse, and
Bryony has special plans to make sure the
coming Christmas will be full of surprises...

Black Cats
Books to pounce on

Spooks Away

SUE PURKISS

"Those who enter Inverscreech should be wary. Those walls contain some deep, dark secrets."

Young ghosts Spooker, Goof and Holly are off to a remote Scottish castle to make a video about how to haunt. But the castle turns out to be less lonely than expected. The arrival of a bunch of Americans and a series of spooky goings on give the ghosts rather more to deal with than they bargained for…

Black Cats
Books to pounce on